I0579914

# Hazardous

Gary Feller

Copyright © 2024 by Gary Feller

All rights reserved.

No portion of this book may be reproduced in any form without written permission from the publisher or author, except as permitted by U.S. copyright law.

# Contents

# Chapter 1: The Daily

Hadera's POV

I slowly wake up to a vibrating bed, yes my bed vibrates, since I can't hear it's the best option for an alarm. I get out of my bed and quickly get ready for school, I brush my teeth, let down my hair, and get dressed in a black skirt and faint pink sweater with black doc martens.

I add a bit of lip gloss to the look and I'm finally done. I walk downstairs to be met with the daily routine of the club, everyone's at the table eating breakfast, talking, laughing, some even drinking, but that's my family for you. *"Good morning honey would you like pancakes?"* Mom asks coming up in front of me. *That's fine wheres Kai?* I ask noticing my brother is gone. *"He's upstairs mind getting him for me?"* Dad says giving me a kiss on my temple. I nod before hurrying off Kai's room. I knock on the door before entering to say my brother was in bed with a half-naked woman, I screamed I'm not sure how loud I did but I guess it was pretty loud since Kai woke up and I could feel a lot of vibrations from down the hall.

"WHAT HAPPENED," Kai screamed as he Got up, at least I think he said that I went off how his lips moved. Soon after my vision was blocked by Dad and Uncle Marcus, Dad led me towards the commons as I still stood shocked at what I saw, my whole face red as I blushed in embarrassment. *"I am forever traumatized,"* I say finally letting myself speak, which I hardly do *" Sorry baby girl I wouldn't have sent you if I had known"* Dad says with a guilty look on his face. As you have probably figured out I am what you would consider innocent in most eyes,  I don't believe I'm that innocent but that's what my family and friend say.

*"It's ok,"* I say getting up to head to my dad's truck, I wait inside till Kai comes out fully dressed to take me to school. You're probably wondering where Judith is, well she's in South Carolina with her dad preparing for the annual chapter get-together we have very few years. This will be the first time I get to go since the last time I didn't want

to go because I was still learning how to communicate with people. *"I'm sorry you had to see that Angel,"* Kai finally says, I can tell he let out a loud sigh. "*It's fine Princey,*" I replied smiling at is altered nickname I gave him. He laughs before buckling in and starting the car.

We soon reach my school, as soon as we reach I could see all the girls gawking over my brother as he opens the car door for me. I climb out of the truck and give Kai a hug before he gets back in the car driving off. I silently walk to my locker, people just staring at me, some with envy some with sympathy, and some with disgust. This is what happens on the Daily, Judith tells me people only look at me like that because they're either sorry for me, envy my beauty, or just don't like me cause they can never be me, her words not mine. As I open my locker I see a bunch of papers fall out of my locker, some big some small but all hold the same messages. Your disgusting, You should Die, Why do you even exist, Deaf Bitch, Freak, Just kill yourself already.

They always held the same message and no matter how much I tell myself they are wrong after so many years of this I started to believe it. I never told anyone about the notes, I probably never will. I pick up the small pile of papers and shove them into an old shoebox I keep in my locker. The shoebox is filled to the brim with notes from over the years but I just keep them as a reminder of all the people that hate me and think I'm useless in the world. The first bell rings and I head off to my first-period class, Math, Math isn't my favorite subject but I guess I do good in it.

Math was boring, the teacher never calls on me since he knows I don't usually talk. My next classes went by like a breeze though and now it was time for lunch. I usually don't each lunch in the cafeteria but today I was feeling confident enough to sit in the cafeteria surrounded by all the people who hate me. I was quietly enjoying my food when a girl named Baily walked up to me with her groupies and started yelling at me but I didn't know what she was saying because her lips were moving too fast. I just continued eating looking away from her when I felt her nails dig into my hand pulling me up out of my seat to face her. I still couldn't understand her but I could tell she was yelling about ignoring someone. Probably me ignoring her, I try to shake my hand from hers but her nails re-anchored into my wrist almost drawing blood.

She continued to yell at me while I stood confused till one of her groupies tapped her should and told her something. Baily looked angrier as she turned to me and punch me right in the face, before I could even create everything went black...

# Chapter 2: Principle Dumbass

I'm just a misunderstood man who has had a past with women. I don't trust women because of my mom but it doesn't stop me from dreaming of having a woman who's perfect for me just like my Uncle Don.

Hazards POV

"Hey, uncle Don what are you doing here?" I ask opening my front door to be met by my uncle and Cousin Judith. "We came to make sure ya'll are still coming for the chapter get-together in a few days," Uncle Don says as they both walk in. "Wouldn't miss it," My dad says from the kitchen as he finishes breakfast. "Who knows what could happen this year I just hope Hadera is ready to be around a lot of unknown people," Judth says stealing a piece of bacon from my plate, giving me a cheeky glare. "Who's Hadera?" Dad asks plating food for all of us "She's My enforcer, Reaper's, Daughter, " Uncle Don replies sitting at the dining table.

"How come we've never met her?" I ask thinking back to the last chapter get-together. "Well she's deaf and at the time of our last get-together she was still learning how to communicate with others," Judith explains while coating her eggs with ketchup. "How long has she been deaf for or was she born deaf?" Dad asks digging into his food. "She was born deaf, and it was caused by her being premature," Uncle Don answers with a sad sigh, I can tell that isn't the full story. "She's my best friend though, she's very adorable and innocent," Judith says giggling at the last part. I wonder what she meant by innocent how innocent could she be...?

Time skip

"You all packed son?" My dad asks from my room doorway. "Yeah almost, what time are we leaving tomorrow?" I ask putting the last few items in my suitcase. "We'll be heading to the compound around noon then probably leave from there an hour or so later, it's only a 3-hour drive to Atlanta, so it's not too far," Replies, I nod thinking he would go away but he stays and says "No funny business when we get there, we don't need you getting arrested while we're there, and please no sleeping around cause next thing you know your sleeping with the wrong person and starting unneeded fights...again." The story he is referring to was when a girl told me she was single and I slept with her but she ended up being a gang leader's girlfriend, so there was a lot of bloodsheds that week. "That was one time, and she lied to me!" I yelled out as my father walked down the hall calling it laughter...

Kai's POV

"Kai I need you to come with me to pick up your sister," Dad says angrily walking out the compound doors. "What happened, is she in trouble?!" I ask a bit frantic since my sister has NEVER broken a rule or thought of it. "No, some girl punched her in the face for no damn reason," Dad says angrily starting up his bike while I start up the truck. Why the hell would someone just punch my sister in the face for no damn reason.

Time Skip

Dad and I stormed into the school faces filled with anger, everyone parting to let us through not wanting to make us any angrier. "Where is my daughter!" Dad yells as he enters the main office, the poor old lady points to the principles office where I see a blond girl barely wearing anything waiting in a chair and I see my little Angel through the window of the door of the principal's office. We walk straight in not even knocking first. "Would you like to explain why my little angel got punched in the face for no damn reason?" My dad asks calmly, a little too calmly. "W-well it seems that your daughter had provoked Miss James," The dumbass principal says stuttering out like a bitch. "How could that possibly be my sister is deaf you dumbass and she hardly ever speaks," said crossing my arms.

"W-well I-I," Principle dumbass stutters around his words while I walk outside and grab the blonde group by the wrist and drag her into the office. "WHAT THE HELL DID YOU DO TO MY SISTER!" I yell at her sitting her on of the chairs. "That bitch was spreading rumors about me and she left horrible notes in my locker!" The bitch yells lying as she had to think for a good 5 minutes before even responding. My sister sat confused as everyone is yelling at each other, "Did you even think to get my daughter's side of the story Principle Dumbass?" Dad asks mad as he hasn't heard anything about Hdera's side of the story.

"N-no," Principle dumbass stutters out, I slam my hand on the table and continued yelling how principle dumbass is dumb and how this blond bimbo is lying. *"Stop it all of you!"* Hadera signs and somewhat yells in her broken English. *"I was just trying to enjoy my lunch when she walked up to me and started yelling at me even though I couldn't hear her so I just ignored her till she grabbed me and punched me,"* Hadera explains. *"Well that should clear up everything I want her suspended and my daughter won't be coming to school for a while,"* Dad says picking up Hadera gently and carrying her out the door with me following behind.

Drakes POV (Time Skip)

*"How's the eye?"* I ask Hadera as Kai sits her down on the couch with an ice pack to her face. *It's fine* She replies putting the ice down to sign and quickly putting it back. Of course, Principle Dumbass didn't think to give her an ice pack so she has a black eye and her eye is all red and irritated. Hadera reaches into her backpack and pulls out her various folders filled with homework, even after being punched in the face she's still thinking about her grades, unlike her brother who would instantly take this time to play video games or watch TV. I walk upstairs to see my beautiful wife swinging around our

bedroom pole, yes we still have a bedroom pole get over it, "I see you still like swinging around on that thing," I say coming up behind her and hugging her.

"It's mostly for exercise now Babe," she replies with a giggle. "When are Prez and Judith supposed to be back?" she asks taking a sip from her water bottle. "They will be back tomorrow evening, then we will have the welcome Party for King and his chapter," I reply helping Aniya get undressed for a shower...

Hadera's POV (Sorry for all the POV changes I promise, last one)

I finished most of my homework for the next two weeks since I won't be going back to school in person for a while. I head up to my room putting away my stuff before rummaging through my gym bag to find the shoebox. I take out the new notes and study all of them slowly taking them into thought. I know I should probably throw them away but I can never bring myself to, the more I read the notes the more I realised how useless I am to the world I can't drive, I can't do certain jobs, I cant do so things that I normal person would be able to do easily. Even though my self-esteem is low it doesn't stop me from dreaming big, I've always wanted to be a musician and I can't say I'm good or not because I've never heard myself sing, only my schools' choir teacher has, she's the one who taught me to sing and play the piano.

Time Skip (Dinner)

*"What the hell happened to you!"* Aunty Dalia signs dramatically and I could tell she was yelling. *I got punched in the face for ignoring a girl I couldn't hear,* I sign shrugging at the end, Aunty Dalia continues to yell but not sign what he's saying so I'm guessing she's saying a string the curse words. *"Calm down babe,"* Uncle Ace says rubbing aunty Dalias back soothingly. I wish I could have a relationship like my aunts and uncles. Even my best friend Judith has a boyfriend and she's younger than me. Most guys tell me it's a turn-off when I tell them I'm deaf so I never expect to have any romantic relations with someone. "*You ok sweetie?*" Aunty Alana asks looking a bit concerned, that's when I realized I was crying. I quickly wiped my tears and nodded giving her a fake smile.

I down in between Dad and Kai and start to eat my food keeping my head down. I felt a tap on my shoulder and I look up to be met with Kai's face laced with concern. *You ok?* he signs not wanting to interrupt everyone's conversations. I node giving him a fake smile, soon I lost my appetite and excused myself for bed. I take my makeup off, take a shower, do skin, care, and climb into bed. I set an alarm for 2 am and lay down thinking of everything that happened today my eyes start to get heavy and soon enough I'm out...

# Chapter 3: Almost Caught



Hadera's POV

I woke up to my vibrating bed, the sun was still down it was about 2 am now. You're probably wondering why I'm waking up so early, well it's the only time the compound is empty with exception of the nighttime guards at the gate. You'd think I would be sneaking out to a party or something right? Well, I'm sneaking around the compound to practice music, and yes my family doesn't know about it. My choir teacher at school, Mrs. Padik, has been teaching me music since freshmen year after she heard me trying to sing and play the piano, based on a video I had seen on youtube. Every month we work on new songs and this month we're trying a bit hard song, Take Me to Church by Hozier.

Many years ago Aunty Emma used to play the piano so we have a grand piano in the backroom of the compound which I secretly cleaned up and restored over the years. Nobody comes into the storage room anymore since they think it's packed to the brim with junk. Let's just say this storage room was very big when I cleaned it out a while back. Since middle school, I've been trying to teach myself Piano so I cleaned it out over time and put in some furniture that I bought with my own money at a thrift shop, I even managed to find some paint in the back shed for the walls.

The room is something like this but a bit more minimalistic and the windows are pretty small with curtains.

I walk as quietly as possible towards the downstairs and behind the bar towards the storage room door. I let out a breath as I finally reached the room setting the door quietly. I turn on the lights and set up my sheet music on the piano. I stretch my fingers and try the voice exercises that Mrs. Padik taught me. After a good 10 minutes of warming up, I start with just playing the piano and trying to feel the correct rhythm. I finally find a rhythm that feels correct so I start from the top and try singing while recording myself to show to Mrs. Padik.

[There should be a GIF or video here. Update the app now to see it.]

After recording about five times I start to feel tired so I look at the time and realized that it was almost 3 am to pack up all my items and head back to my room. On my way back to my room I see one of the bathroom lights on so I sit on the steps and try to act like I doing homework on my sheet music. Soon I feel the vibrations of a door closing and a hand touch my shoulder,m*What are you doing up so early* Uncle Ace signs not wanting to wake anyone up. *I woke up and wasn't tired so I decided to get something to drink then do my homework,* I sign back showing him my binder and giving him a sheepish smile. Uncle Ace hesitantly nods about to turn away when I run off to my room, Not suspicious whatsoever, I shut my bedroom door and slide my back down setting my music binder down, let's just get some sleep.

3rd person POV

Ace stood there dumbfounded, he had never seen Hadera act too secretive and nervous he could tell she was lying, but Hadera never lied. He was about to turn away when he saw a paper on the floor where Hadera was sitting. He picked up the paper and was confused to be met with sheet music, as far as he knew Hadera has never touched a musical instrument, and as far as he knew we didn't own any musical instruments. Ace made his way back to his bedroom where his sleeping wife lay soundly asleep.

Time Skip

Everyone woke up excited the next morning for the welcome party that would be hosted later that day. But one specific member lay in his bed confused about why his niece would blatantly lie to his face last night. Ace walked downstairs, everyone was drinking coffee and talking about the events that would take place later tonight. "Do we have any musical instruments here?" I ask out of nowhere as I take a sip of my coffee. "Umm I don't think so," Reaper says rubbing the back of his neck. "We have a piano actually in the backroom, why?" Emma says cleaning up the kitchen counter. "Well last night I was using the bathroom-" Ace started but was cut off by Dalia.

"Babe no one wants to hear your bathroom stories!" Dalia says smacking him in the back of his head. "That's not what I was going to say, last night I saw Hadera sneaking back upstairs with a binder when I asked what she was doing she said homework and I knew she lied because of A. It was almost 3 am and B. She has never lied and is very bad at it, after she said that she ran to her room and locked the door but what she didn't realize was that she had dropped her paper and it was sheet music," Ace finally finishes breathless putting the paper on the table for everyone to see.

"That is a bit weird since she's never touched an instrument but it's impossible for her to play that piano it's been buried behind storage room junk for years," Emma says biting a piece of bacon. "Why don't you'll just ask her when she wakes up like normal people," Ace's son, Dario, says in a duh voice. "Or pull up the video storage from the storage room," Damien says getting down Hacker's laptop on the kitchen counter. "That's a good idea," Ace says giving the computer to Hacker, He sighs before pulling up all the past camera feed from the storage room. "See nothing the storage closet is as musty as ever," Hacker says showing everyone the video feed. "Then what was she doing downstairs with sheet music, if she wanted to study sheet music then why would she need to be downstairs," Emma says a bit confused. *"Morning"* They all turn shocked to see Hadera cheerfully skipping into the kitchen grabbing a piece of bacon. Everyone signs morning back to her. *Why are you all staring did I do something wrong?*Hadera asks with a worried look on her face.

*"No Angel we just have never seen you so cheerful in the morning,"* Drake says *Oh, my art teacher wants me to come and help her at school today* Hadera signs back anxiously. They all could tell she was lying because of A. She was bad at lying and B. She doesn't take art. *"Ok, Angel do you need someone to drop you off?"* Drake asks going along with her lie. *That would be fine* Hadera signs back letting out a sigh of relief. Hadera was so nervous and she felt bad for lying to her family but she didn't want them to know yet. Mrs. Padik had emailed her early that morning wanting her to come to the schools' choir performance to be an opener. Mrs. Padlik thought it would be a good message for people to see someone who is deaf following their dreams.

Hadera packed her black choir dress into her gym back and a pair of plain black heels. As soon as Hadera was done she went downstairs and Drake drove her to the school. Drake didn't trust what Hadera was saying so he followed her inside the school. Drake kept his distance from Hadera but what confused him was that she walked straight into a room marked music room. Drake wasn't the only parent there, there were many parents dressed in suits and dressed

waiting in the auditorium. Drake was confused maybe his daughter

was stagehand or maybe a lights person. Oh, how he had no clue how

amazing his daughter was...

# Chapter 4: Take a Bow

A /n-Hadera's dress

Hadera's POV

I have never been more excited and nervous in my life, *Are you ready?* Mrs. Padik asks giving me a huge smile. I nod returning a smile, Mrs. Padik thought it would be better for me to sing a song that I knew by heart so I had less chance of messing up since I have a fear of embarrassing myself by talking. So the song ill be singing is Million To One by Camilla Cabello, it's the only song I can sing without messing up instantly. *Ok, some of the other choir kids will be doing the music for you so all you have to do is sing, I know you can do it* Mrs. Padik signs as she leads me to the stage wings. I could tell some of the choir kids were looking at me weirdly since I had my shoes off, for some context I use the vibrations from the music to sing, and it's easier to feel them when y shoes are off.

*"Welcome Everyone to the Colombus Highschool Advanced Choir showcase I am the choir director, Mrs. Padik, Before we get to our main choir we will be showcasing a few students on their musical talent, as you can see I've been singing this whole time because one of our openers is Deaf, I would like to welcome our Opener Hadrea Keita-Stone,"* Mrs. Padik says motioning me to come on stage. I walk onto stage nervously *Why don't you introduce yourself I'll be in the audience,* Mrs. Padik says walking down to the front row of seats that are reserved for the showcase acts. *"H-Hello, M-my name is Hadera I-I was born Deaf in both ears a-and I'm going to be s-singing Million To One by Camilla C-Cabello"* I stutter out stepping away from the mic and looking behind me to see some of the choir kids setting up their instruments.

[There should be a GIF or video here. Update the app now to see it.]

I take some deep breaths before I feel the music start, once I started singing it was like all my nerves disappeared and all the bad thoughts in my head stopped. When I finished singing I opened my eyes to see everyone standing and clapping I look down at Mrs. Padik and she signed *Take a Bow.* I bowed as the tears fell from my eyes. I can't believe I got a standing ovation! The more I looked around the more my mood dimmed, I wish my parents were here, even if it was just one of them I wish they were here. I made my way off the stage and into the wings of the stage. Everyone in the choir room was clapping in ASL (It kind of looks like slow jazz hands) Seeing them clap for me made me smile again. Eventually, all the opening performances were done and it was time for the choir to sing, Mrs. Padik liked throwing different songs some in different languages and some with different cultures, so this year's showcase song is Baba Yetu which is a prayer song in Swahili. Good luck to them and good luck to me explaining why I came to school even though I don't take art...

[There should be a GIF or video here. Update the app now to see it.]

Drakes POV

Seeing my daughter sing was probably the most heartwarming moment ever. I just want to know why she didn't tell us about her passion for music. I may or may not have recorded the whole thing, can you blame me my daughter is amazing. I quickly made my way to the nearest grocery store and bought her flowers.

Time Skip

By the time I had gotten back the main choir had finished so I waited in the hallway for Hadera. *Dad your here early!* Hadera signed shock evident on her face as she probably realized she still has her dress on. *I know I'm early but I got these for you,* I sign backhanding her the flowers. *Thank you, Dad you didn't have to* she signs with a smile on her face as she gives me a side hug trying not to hit me with the flowers. *But I wanted to, you were amazing out there* I sign kissing her forehead. *You're not mad?* She signs surprised, *Why would I be you are amazing, but I'm a bit hurt you didn't tell me,* I sign back as we walk outside to the truck. Hadera explains her reasoning which I understand why she would be nervous she never likes speaking.

We drive back to the compound Hadera still admiring the flowers I got her. As we reached the compound I see two times the usual amount of motorcycles in front of the main building letting me know that King and his club have arrived. Hadera didn't look fazed at all the new bikes, I'm guessing she found out about the chapter get-together. As soon as I parked Hadera jumped out of the car rushing inside, I'm guessing to get changed before someone sees her.

I take her bag out of the back seat and set it on one of the couches in the lounge room. I head to the meeting room since Prez called church almost 30 minutes ago and I'm late. "Look who decided to show up!" Prez dramatically says as I enter the room. "I got caught up with something," I reply nonchalantly giving him a clipped answer. "Where the hell were you that your this late to church!" Ace yells out getting a little too close to me. "Oh, I'm sorry I was just trying to get to the bottom of Hadera's lying situation cause you were overly concerned," I say pushing him away.

"Woah Woah Woah! You'll need to calm your tits!" King yells as he and Prez separate us. "Oh, and it took you a whole 30 minutes to ask her what she was doing?" Rusty asks, "She's been hiding the fact that she been taking choir and piano lessons from us and I stayed and watched her performance at school then I drove, got some, flowers and gave them to her and we talked about her little secret then we came straight here happy?" I reply frustrated and mad at myself for exposing my daughter's secret for the sake of not getting my ass whooped.

"She what? But that doesn't explain why she was sneaking around at 3 am," Hacker says "Hey when did ya'll clean out the storage room?"

we hear Dario yell from the hallway. We all speed towards Dario as he's in the old storage room. "Damn this place is clean as hell!" Kai says as he steps in. "This makes no sense the cameras show that the room is still musty as ever," Hacker says pulling up the camera feed again. "If I didn't know any better I would say your little girl has a few more secrets and if not she is a witch," King says walking around the room. *"What are you doing in there your not supposed to be in here, D-Dario, don't touch that!"* We hear a Haderas small voice say from behind us. Before Hadera could reach Dario he had already touched the top of the piano and it dropped on his fingers...

Hadera's POV

After getting dressed I could feel pounding footsteps downstairs so me being me I gingerly walk behind the bar to see a crowd of men going into my music room. *"What are you doing in there your not supposed to be in here, D-Dario, don't touch that!"* I try and yell seeing Dario touch the top of my piano. Before I could reach him the top falls smashing his fingers. "AHHHHHHHHH FUCK ME!" Dario yells and this is the first time I can tell what someone is saying. Some of the unknown men lift the piano top off his fingers. Dad runs to get Aunty Alana while I stand there as the men turn to look at me,

I sheepishly smile walking over to the piano probing the top back up and fixing everything that they ha touched.

*"So you play the piano?"* Uncle Don asks, I nod before sitting down at the piano and playing a small portion from taking me to church. *"That was amazing why don't you go to the common room and then we can introduce everyone to you,"* Uncle don recommends. Time to meet everyone...

# Chapter 5: Crush

Samuels POV

It took about 3 hours to reach Uncle Don's compound, as soon as we got there he called Church to introduce us to the prospects and any other new members. "Where the hell is Reaper?!" Uncle Don asked looking around for an answer. "He went to drop off Hadera at school or something half an hour ago," Ace replies. Everyone talked amongst themselves for half an hour till someone barged into the room. "Look who decided to show up!" Prez dramatically says "I got caught up with something," Reaper replies nonchalantly. "Where the hell were you that your this late to church!" Ace yells at him getting in his face.

"Oh, I'm sorry I was just trying to get to the bottom of Haderas lying situation cause you were overly concerned," Reaper replies almost pushing Ace on his ass. They continue to fight till Uncle Don and my dad break them up, Reaper explains where he's been but as soon as he finished we hear another man yell "Hey when did ya'll clean out the storage room?" Everyone looked shocked except for my dad and my cause as far as we're concerned that's a music room, not a storage closet.

"Damn this place is clean!" Kai says as he walks in. The man who had called at first was touching the grand piano when we heard a small voice that sounded like a miniature yell say, *"What are you doing in there your not supposed to be in here, D-Dario, don't touch that!"* It was too late because Dario had already smashed his fingers when the piano closed. "AHHHH FUCK ME!" he screams in pain as some men lift the top to get his fingers out. They lead a screaming Dario out of the room while a small girl walks in. She was pretty short compared to me probably only 5'2 or 5'3 she had light brown skin and black twisted hair, she was wearing a white skirt and an oversized pink hoodie that had a small pink and white cow, and said Strawberry Cow. I would be lying if I said she wasn't beautiful she was better than beautiful she was gorgeous.

It was like I was in a trans cause next thing you know everyone is walking out of the room and towards the lounge. Everyone filed into the lounge so we could be introduced to the girl in the pink sweater Uncle don introduced my dad, Jesus, and all of our other members that came today. *"And lastly we have Hadera, shes Aniya and Reaper's daughter as well as Kai's sister, she is also deaf and doesn't like talking much,"* Uncle Don says as she gets up and gives my dad and Jesus handshakes when she gets to me she freezes and stares at me. I wink at her and smile at her and I could see a coat of blush staining her cheeks. She lets go of my hand when I look up I'm met with a guy about my age who looks similar to Hadera. "If you touch my sister you'll be sorry," He threatens before following his sister to the other side of the room.

I head to the bar with the rest of the men as the women sit in a booth with Hedera. "That was introduction you had their boy," Jesus says slapping me on the back with a beer in his other hand. "It was nothing," I say casually. "Hazard a blind man could see that the girl has a bit of a crush on you," Jesus says in a duh voice. "What's with you and my daughter?" Reaper asks taking a swig from his beer. "Nothing sir," I say as respectfully as I can, "Where the hell did 'Sir' come from," My dad asks chuckling at me...

Hadera's POV

I may or may not have a crush on Hazard but it's justified I mean look at him he's handsome. *"Who's got you blushing?"* Aunty Emma asks nudging me *Nothing absolutely nothing* I sign a bit too quickly for her liking because she continues to say *"I think our innocent angle has a little crush."* The rest of my aunts and my mom turned in surprise at hearing this. "*No way we have been trying to get this girl to go on a date for years, who is the lucky guy?*" My mom asks making my mouth drop. Was she looking for potential guys for me to date? *MOM* I sign my whole face completely turning red.

*"Honey your getting older, you need more social interaction, especially with guys who don't practically live with you"* Mom says trying to get me to compromise but I'm not having it *"NO, I DON'T NEED YOU MEDDLING IN MY SOCIAL LIFE, NOT AGAIN"* I yell storming up to my room and slamming my door. You're probably thinking why is this girl so dramatic but I'm not the last time mom tried meddling in my supposed social life it ended with me going home crying because a girl who I supposedly was friends with told me she was only friends with me because my mom bribed her.

Reaper's POV

All of us men sat around the bar nursing beers till we hear yelling from the other side of the room. *"NO, I DON'T NEED YOU MEDDLING IN MY SOCIAL LIFE, NOT AGAIN,"* my daughter yells at her mother as she storms upstairs slamming her door. "What the hell just happened?" King asks as we all look at the Old lady Booth. I can see Aniya regretted whatever she had said to Hadera. "I'll go check on them," I say setting my beer down and walking over to the girl's booth. "What happened?" I ask hugging a crying wife, "I-I just want her to be more social with people her age, I didn't mean to make her think I was going to do something like I did last time with Janessa," Aniya sobs out, I instantly get mad just thinking of that horrible girl Janessa all she ever wanted was to make Hadera's life a living hell so she took the chance when Aniya asked her to befriend Hadera.

"Don't worry ill talk to her," I say giving her a soft kiss on the lips making the other Old Ladies 'aww' I glare at them and make my downstairs. I try opening Haderas door but it turns out she finally wanted to use her lock. I ring the room doorbell that notifies her when someone is at the door by flashing a light. I wait a few seconds and as I was about to ring it again she slips a piece of paper and pen under the door that says 'Go away mom' I take the paper and pen and write down 'It's dad' as soon as she took the note she let me in. *She sent you up here didn't she* Hadera signs, *No, I wanted to talk to you, you know your mom isn't intentionally trying to pry* I sign back to her sitting on her desk chair as she sits on the bed.

*I know but why can't she just leave me alone I'm happy with Judith* she signs letting out a sigh, *Your mom just wants to see you happy* I sign back to her, *Dad you don't understand she thinks I have a crush on someone and now all the girls know and there just gonna try and me to go on a date* She signs rather quickly. Wait for Crush? Date? Oh hell Nah! *Well...do you want to go on a date with this person?* I ask a bit scared of the answer. *I don't know dad I just met him, and iv never been on a date people don't like that I'm deaf* she signs with a sad expression on her face.

I hate that these little boys running around think my daughter is incapable of being a good girlfriend just cause she is deaf. *It doesn't matter what they say sweetheart if they love you they'll love you disabled or not,* I sign before getting up to hug her. We stay in a hugging position for a while till I hear soft snores coming from the small body in my arms. I set her down in bed and tuck her in, I miss

tucking her in like this it's been too long, and it's a reminder that she's

getting older, and maybeI'lll start allowing her to date or maybe in

like 5 years. AS long as she's happy...

# Chapter 6: Aunty Flo and An Almost Ass Beating

Hazard's POV\

After everything that happened yesterday, everyone thought it would be a good idea to just have a relaxing day. Mostly everyone left the compound the girls all went to the spa and most of the men went to a local shooting range or the hardware store. I on the other hand stayed behind since no one was gonna be here at the compound I could do whatever I wanted in peace. I was enjoying the silence when I saw a small figure out of the corner of my eye. It was Hadera she looked as if she was uncomfortable. She walked around the room towards the kitchen not even noticing I'm there, I guess she assumed everyone was gone.

I slowly walk up behind her and tapped her shoulder, she almost tripped seeing me. After seeing me she almost instantly froze upon seeing me. *"H-hi"* she says softly regaining her composer "Hi," I say slowly so she can read my lips, *"I thought everyone left"* she says turning around bending down to open the freezer, I could feel her ass rub against cock making groan as I could feel myself get hard. I move away from her hoping she didn't feel anything but I guess I was wrong because she turned around, when she looked up at me I could see her face had gone completely red. *"Um I-I'm sorry,"* she says trying the walk away before she can exit the kitchen I grab her wrist pulling her into my chest "Don't be sorry," I say to her hoping she understands.

I didn't know someone's face could get even redder than hers, she looked like a tomato. As if something scared her she ran away upstairs...

Hadera's POV

I woke up today hoping to have a happy day but no I was met with a bloody morning. And to make my day even worse I only had one small pad left and my period is heavy on the first few days, Since no one is here I have no one to drive to the store. I don't want to interrupt the girl's spa day so I just walk downstairs and grab some comfort food. As I was facing the fridge I felt a hand on my shoulder making me jump. I turn round to be met with Hazard and his deliciously handsome face, *"H-Hi"* I say blush coating my cheeks. "Hi," he says back slowly probably wanting me to be able to read his lips. I turn around quickly grabbing a small tub of ice cream from the freezer. When I bent down I had felt something touch my butt. I stand up turning around glancing down to see something I never want to see again.

I quickly look up at Hazard who had moved away slightly, I look up my face probably tomato red I quickly apologize then try and hurry away trying to get to the door when Hazar grabs my wrist pulling me into his chest. "Don't be sorry," he says giving me his natural smirk. I feel something running down my leg so I quickly run upstairs Hazard on my tail. I run straight into the bathroom to even close my room door in the process. I quickly tried cleaning myself off but I still needed a pad. In my peripheral vision, I see a pen and paper being pushed under the door. 'Are you ok?!' it read I'm guessing it's Hazard, I give in so I grab the pen and paper and write 'I started my period but I don't have anything for it at the moment' and slid it under the door.

I didn't get a reply so I just sat in the bathroom for almost half an hour, after a while I started crying thinking about how bad my day has been. Just as all hope was lost the paper came from under the door saying 'Can you open the door?' I pull up my pants not caring at this point and open the door to reveal Hazard holding a bag with two boxes inside. He hands me the bag and closes the door, I look in the bag to see tampons and pads. I quickly clean myself up with the extra clothes I keep in my bathroom. I step out of the bathroom finally all clean and comfortable, Hazard was sitting on my bed waiting for me. 'Everything ok?' he has written on a paper, I nod climbing into my bed trying not to blush from embarrassment ' I'll back give me a second' write on the same piece of paper coming back with two bags one filled with candy and chips, the other had Mcdonalds. I almost started crying from everything he had gotten me. "Thank you," I say quietly as jump up to hug him.

He seemed surprised by the hug but I guess he doesn't get them often. I break the hug and pat the spot next to me. I guess he got the message because he climb into bed with me lifting me onto his lap and making me squeal. We sat in the same position eating and watching a movie occasionally speaking to each other. After a while I noticed Hazard fall asleep, I shut off the TV and slowly but surely I fell asleep next to him...

Judith's POV

"So is it just me or do ya'll ship Hazard and Hadera," I say causing all the girls to turn their heads and look in my direction including Aunty Emma who was in the middle of an eyebrow wax. "I mean I did confront her on her little crush on him cause she was blushing pretty hard after talking to him yesterday," Emma says shrugging it off like it's nothing. "Girls listen to yourself this Hadera we are talking about she blushes even when someone signs a curse word maybe he said something and one of the guys signed it and she blushed at that," Dalia says trying to reason with us. "I think they'd make a cute couple, I mean she reminds me of me falling in love with her father in a way," Aniya says smiling at the thought of her past. "Maybe this will help Hadera get out of her shell," I say happily hoping my best friend will finally break out of his little shell.

After our little trip to the spa, we head back to the compound upon entering the compound all we could hear was yelling and the sound of crying. All the men were yelling at Hazard or each other and Hadera sat in a corner crying, she didn't know what was happening since no one even thought to explain the situation to her. "WHAT THE HELL IS GOING ON!" Aunty Emma yells as Aunty Aniya is trying to break up a fight between Uncle Drake and Uncle Dean. "THE HELL WAS YOUR SON DOING WITH MY DAUGH-TER!" Uncle Drake yells as Aniya and Emma finally get all the men to stop. I make my way around everyone trying to get over to Hadera to consult with her, she was shaking with anger but she was also still crying.

"I WASN'T DOING ANYTHING WITH HER I WAS TRYING TO HELP HER DAMN IT!" Hazard yells in Uncle Drake's face causing him to get a hard punch to his face making him collapse to the ground. I could see anger overtake Hadera's face, I have never seen her so angry, I guess she could tell what Uncle Drake said because she started yelling at him *" HE DIDN'T DO ANYTHING HE

HELPED ME!"* Hadera grabbed Hazard's hand, helped him up, and lead him towards the infirmary room we were all dumbfounded.

"ANYONE WANNA TELL US WHAT THE HELL JUST HAP- PEN!" Aunty Aniya yells unbuckling her belt and folding it into a murderous weapon.

"I came home to see my daughter and I find her in bed with HIS son," Uncle Drake says looking t Uncle Dean with rage in his eyes. "Did any of you think to ask Hadera what happened?" I asked glaring at them. No one answered my question so I got my answer, "Ya'll know Hadera never lies about shit like this, and yall didn't even think to ask her what happened!" I start my voice slowly getting louder and louder. "AND IF ANY OF YALL ARE MARRIED TO ANYONE OF US YOUR SLEEPING ON THE COUCH, THAT INCLUDES YOU DAMIEN!" I yell flipping all the men off, all my aunts agreeing with me walking upstairs, leaving blankets and pillows on the floors outside.

Hadera's POV

*"I'm sorry about them,"* I say putting a butterfly bandage on a small cut right under his eyebrow. "It's ok," he replies, I take one of the icepacks out of the freezer gently putting it over his down bruised eye.

*"We match now,"* I say taking one of the wet cloths and wiping the concealer off my eye to reveal my black eye from when Baily punished me. I could see his eyes widen, he was about to say something when I cut in *"Don't worry, a girl at school punched me when I ignored her, but I couldn't exactly hear her."* He only nods somewhat relieved...

3rd Person POV

All the married men had messed up, they were all sleeping on the couch downstairs that night. Even Damien slept on the couch since Judith refused to let him into HIS room. Almost all the men that were in love slept downstairs, what I mean by almost was Hazard didn't sleep alone that night he slept in Hadera's bed per request. Her excuse for letting him stay there that night was that she claimed she wanted to keep an eye on him, oh she sure had her eyes on him alright...

# Chapter 7: The Notes

Hazard's POV

After everything that had happed yesterday I could tell everyone was feeling guilty. Reaper had apologized early this morning after talking to Hedrea. Since the last 2 days have been crazy everyone decided we would have our annual party tonight, so that's how I ended up here in the lounge room hanging onto a rope for dear life. "I KNOW I SAID I WOULD HELP BUT SERIOUSLY WHY AM I HANGING FROM THE CEILING," I yelled at everyone as they laughed at my franticness. "We needed you to hang some stuff but you kicked the latter down," Dad said throwing his head back cackling. "JUST GET ME DOWN," I yell trying my best to not fall to my death. Eventually the fuckers got the ladder and got me down.

As everyone continued getting ready for the party I managed to sneak away. I walked down the halls exploring the compound's different rooms. I stopped at the room that I went to the first day I came here Hadrea's music room. I could hear music coming from the room, I slowly opened the door to reveal Hadera playing her piano and singing...

Hadrea's POV (Warning- mention of Bullying )

While everyone was getting ready for the party I sat in my music room playing random tunes. My eyes were soon drawn to the box on one of my shelves, the box of notes. I stand up reach for the box and grab it setting it on the bench next to me. I review all the notes, they always said the same thing You're ugly, your useless, disabled freak, ugly pig, why can't you disappear, freak, kill yourself. Why can't I just be normal like the other kids, I'm deaf, I'm different. But I like being different, I smile thinking of all the things that I've accomplished. They're jealous because even though I'm disabled I've become for successful than they have ever been. I quickly open my binder looking through the pages till I land on a song that has saved me more than anyone or anything, Perfect by P!ink.

[There should be a GIF or video here. Update the app now to see it.]

I'm using this as a reference but you can use another stripped cover

I sing slowly trying not to mess up the song, I was startled as I finished seeing Hazard standing in front of the door clapping. *"What are you doing in here?!"* I ask quickly trying to put the box notes back on the shelf but I guess God had other plans for me cause I ended up dropping the box spilling all derogatory notes on the floor. Hazard quickly runs over to help me pick up the notes, right as I was about the grab the last note he picked it up and I guess he saw what was on it cause his face turned into a rageful expression.

"W-what are these?" he asks taking more of the notes out and opening them. *"T-they're nothing just some notes from classmates,"* Is says trying to take the notes from his hand. He picks up the box rushing out the door and into the lounge where everyone is. *"Give those back they aren't yours,"* I say trying to stop Hazard, I tackled him causing him to stagger and drop the box right onto one of the tables that just so happened to be the table my family sat at. *"What's going on with you two?"* Uncle Don asks annoyed as one of the notes managed to get in his scotch glass. "You wanna tell them or should I!" Hazard says I'm guessing angrily, I shake my head looking down avoided everyone's gaze...

## Hazard's POV

"I was helping her clean up all these pieces of paper when they dropped in her music room and when I looked at the papers they were small notes saying how she was useless, ugly, and she should kill herself, she tried to tell me they were just some notes from some classmates trying to brush it off," I explain taking small glances at Hadrea, by the time I had finished explaining everyone was listening and Hadreas family had already read the notes. Her mom and aunts were in tears, her dad, brother, and uncle's faces held anger and pain in their eyes. I look to my right upon hearing small sobs, Hadreas sobs, she quickly ran upstairs and slammed her door leaving everyone silent...

# Chapter 8: Weed and Dresses

Hazard's POV

Everyone stood in silence as Hadera ran upstairs, all I could do was stare at the notes laying on the wooden table. "W-who could say such things to her," Aniya choked out sobbing into Reaper's chest, "I-I don't know, I doubt Hadera would have told if I hadn't shown you," I say sadly scooping the notes up and putting them back int her box. "The kids at school always do it, Hadera didn't want ya'll to worry so she told me to keep it a secret," Judith suddenly says, her voice hoarse trying to hold back tears. "Sweetheart you know better than to keep something like this a secret," Aunty Emma says putting a comforting hand on her daughter's shoulder. "I know but she had something to hold over my head so I didn't want to snitch, I don't even know how she found out!" Judith yelled out exasperated, then quickly realized what she had said. "What could she have had over your head for you not to tell your family what happened," My dad asked curiously. "There isn't a point in hiding it now," Uncle Don says crossing his arms, Aunty Emma following in stance.

"Fine! She found out that I had been smoking joints behind the school with a couple of other kids," Judith answers, her voice gradually getting quiet and quieter. "YOU WHAT," We all yell staring at her shocked. "Where the hell did you get weed from?!" Kai asks staring at his not so angelic cousin. "WHY ARE YOU YELLING AT ME KAI I GOT THE WEED FROM YOUR ROOM!" Judith yells waving her arms around. That shut Kai up real quick because Aniya started folding her belt up and landed a hard smack to Kai's ass. "OWW," He says rubbing his now possible bruised butt, "I'm gonna go check in Hadera," he says quickly running before his mom can whoop him again...

Hadera's POV

I now lay in bed crying until my heart is content, I didn't want my parents to know, let alone my whole family. I must look like a disappointment in their eyes, a weak, useless, disappointment. My thoughts were interrupted by a flash of light coming from my doorbell. Whoever it was didn't care if I answered because they came in anyway. I felt a soft tap on my shoulder for the person trying to get my attention, I slowly open my eyes and look up to see my brother standing there with a mixed look of sadness and sympathy. *You know we all love you, right?* he asks taking a seat in front of me at my desk. I nod my head signing, *I didn't want ya'll to worry I'm not as helpless as most think.* *We know you are not helpless but it's our job to worry,* Kai signs back.

We continue to talk more, and I ended up telling him everything, the notes, the bullying, and all my little secrets. *So how did you manage to hack the cameras in your music room so t looked like a musty closet?* he asks, his final question. *I spent most of my days hiding in Uncle Marcus's computer room, I picked up most of the things he does,* I answer sitting up from my bed, standing ready to go.

We walk downstairs where everyone was discussing different things, as soon as everyone spotted me they stopped their conversations. I explained everything to everyone, I finally came clean after so many years of secrets. To say most of the club was shocked would be an understatement. Dad and mom came to an agreement that they didn't want me in that school anymore so now I'm to be homeschooled or do online. I agreed to online and then went to find Judith.

I walked into the hallway searching for Judith when I found her and Damien sucking each other's faces off. I attempt to clear my throat looking down avoiding their eyes, they instantly stop and Judith pushes Damien off as if nothing happened. "*C-can you help me get ready for tonight?*" I ask Judith only looking up to get her response. "*YES, Finally I can dress you up, ima makes you look sexy as hell!*" She says excitedly grabbing my arm and dragging me to her room, sitting me on her bed. *Ok I have three options for you!* she signs pretty big which means she would be yelling if she was talking.

*I don't know they are all pretty revealing,* I sign looking at the supposed dresses that remind me more of lingerie. *Why don't I bring Hazard in here and have him choose,* she signs back wiggling her eyebrows. My eyes widen as she starts screaming, probably for hazard. "What happened!" Hazard yells running into the room drawing his gun. My eyes widen as he points the gun around until his eyes land on me. "*Hadera doesn't know what dress to pick, mind helping her out,*" Judith signs winking at me, I pout as I feel my face heat up.

They talk for a second and then Hazard leaves, not before sending me a smile showing off his pearly whites. *He said for you to wear the last dress* Judith says handing me the white mesh long sleeve dress. I slip off my clothes, including my bra, and slip on the dress not caring that Judith is in the room. What we're both girls and we're those kinds of besties. I turn around to find Judith in a red dress that is pretty revealing in my opinion but she looks amazing. *You look so cute,* she signs as she signals for me to do a turn. *You look amazing,* I say blushing as I look at myself in the mirror.

We continue to get ready, Judith doesn't our makeup and hands me a pair of heels. Let's hope this doesn't end like my first homecoming when I fell and broke my ankle wearing heels, that was a dark night. She does a darker makup look on herself, while she did a softer more natural look on me. Soon after we finish getting ready Judith gets a text saying that everyone will be heading to the party at my brothers club since they didn't get to finish decorating the clubhouse. We had Damien drive us since he was the last person at the club house, here goes nothing...

Judith's heels and makeup inspo

Hadera's heels and makeup inspo

# Chapter 9: The Golden Queen and Gunshots

Hazard's POV

After Judith asked me to choose Hadera's dress I couldn't wait to see her in it, Hadera is one of the most gorgeous girls I have ever seen. I had planned to ask her out tonight, I had asked Reaper for permission to take her out after shit hit the fan with the notes this morning. It was much harder than it looked asking him for permission, you know what let's take a trip down memory lane...

Flashback (This afternoon)

"I know this may not be the ideal time to ask this but can I have your permission to take Hadera out on a date?" I ask trying my best to seem confident, looking Reaper in the eyes. "What makes you think you deserve to date my daughter?" He asks menacingly calm, not what I was expecting. "I can protect her better than any other man outside of the club, and you know me, you know my family, what better than the let your daughter date someone who you can trust." Reaper dotes on my answer for a while then finally comes to conclusions. "If you can beat me in a fight then you can ask Hadera on a date, I'm not promising a yes from her but I am promising my blessing," Reaper replies. I nod and he leads me to a gym with a boxing ring. No one followed us in fearing what would happen to me. We hopped into the ring and as I prepared to fight, I would be lying if I said I wasn't scared, Reaper is way taller, muscular, and well trained compared to me. Reaper ready his stance and as he was about to throw a punch he started laughing. I stand confused looking at the laughing giant in front of me. "Did you think I would bet your ass because you want to make my daughter happy? Hadera really likes you and I'm only giving you chance because I know she likes you," Reaper says putting a hand on my shoulder. I go over the basic rules of dating his daughter no touching, no kissing, no funny business, and the most important rule, no hurting her in any way...

Flashback over

As I continued to reminisce my old memories I was interrupted by the doors of the club opening to reveal the rest of the club entering. Soon enough almost everyone was inside except for Judith, Hadera, and Damien. I started to get anxious not knowing if Hadera was even coming tonight or if she was staying home with Judith. I made my way to the bar, ordering a few shots and preparing myself to ask the girl that I like out on a date.

About half an hour passed before Hadera, Judith, and Damien walked through the doors. Hadera was wearing the dress I chose for her, and she looked stunning, the white made her look like an angel from heaven. "Wow," I whisper looking at her as she makes her way toward me. She waves sitting on the stool next to me ordering just a coke. I tap on her shoulder to get her attention before saying "You look beautiful." I could tell she was blushing after my compliment, "*Thank you, you don't look too bad yourself,*" she replies giving me a sweet smile. We continue to talk and laugh, sharing different stories about our families. "Would you like to dance?" I ask offering my hand to her. She agrees and I lead her into the middle of the dance floor. We danced for what felt like hours to AC/DC, We were enjoying ourselves until I heard a bang, I instantly knew it was gunshots...

Hadera's POV

We were just having fun when everyone started scrambling around trying to find hiding places. Hazard tackled me to the ground shielding my body with his. Soon the gunshots stopped and I could feel Hazard moving on top of me but he didn't make any move to get off of me. I roll from under him and check to see if he's alright but all I could do is freeze in fear. He had two gunshot wounds on his back, I quickly rip part of my dress and use the cloth to try and stop the bleeding. King, Uncle Don, and Dad run over picking up Hazard as I'm still applying pressure to his wounds, Aunty Alana following behind us probably addressing his wounds and figuring out what she will need to do to get them out.

Tears were streaming down my face the tears blinding my sight but no matter what I wouldn't let my hands move. I sat in the back of our club van as we made our way back to the clubhouse. As soon as we got to the clubhouse we already had prospects ready with a gurney for Hazard. The men help move him steadily onto the bed and we wheel him into the infirmary. "*Hadera you need to let go Aunty Alana needs to get the bullets out,*" Kai signs to me as we continue into the infirmary. I shake my head more tears streaming down my face. I didn't want to let go, I didn't want them to bleed out and die. I continue shaking my head no "I-I c-can't," I say stuttering, Kai shakes his head and walks behind me trying to pull me away from the hazard. I continue to sob as he carries me away, towards the bar area. I cry into Kai's shoulder as he continues to hold me trying to hush my sobs, but it didn't work all I wanted right now was Samual Hazard DeMarco...

# Chapter 10: *Would you go on a date with me*

H adera's POV

I couldn't stop crying, in that moment seeing Samual minutes from death just ignited that feeling that I couldn't shake off when I first met him. Samual stole my heart the minute I saw him, he's the man I want to be with for the rest of my life. I felt a tap on my shoulder pulling me out of my thoughts, "*He's out of surgery and awake,*" Aunty Alana says making her way to the bar. I stand up quickly making my way toward the infirmary. As I enter I see Samual laying on the bed his guys open, looking straight at me.

"*Y-your ok,*" I say right before hugging him quickly and gently trying not to hurt him. "Of course I'm ok," He says putting a soothing hand on my cheek. "You still look beautiful even with my blood on you, and your makeup messed up," he says, I can tell he laughed at the end. I didn't realize until now that I didn't change out of my bloody clothes nor had I taken off my makeup, I probably had mascara running down my face. I blush as he continues to stare at me with a small smile. I was about the say something when surprisingly he started signing to me...

Samual's POV (Hazard)

Even with her discarded appearance she still looked like a beautiful angel, I could tell she was embarrassed because of her appearance but I didn't care. I could tell she was about the talk when I stopped her by starting to sign myself, "*Will you go on a date with me tomorrow?*" I ask hoping I signed the correct words. She sat there shocked, ever since I laid my eyes on her I've been trying to learn ASL so it would be easier to understand. She slowly started nodding her head her mouth and eyes still wide. "You should close your mouth before you catch flies," I say putting two fingers under her chin, and closing her mouth.

Hadera helps me out of the bed leading me to the bar and helping me sit down, leaving towards the women's table shortly after. As I sit down all the men greet me and Reaper, my dad, and Uncle Don, give me knowing looks. "So looks like someone got a date!" Uncle Don says rather loud so most of the men heard. "Who's the lucky girl?" Kai asks obliviously taking a sip of his beer, "Your sister," I answer cockily giving him a smirk. I could tell Kai was livid as he walked over to me held the collar of my shirt and gave me the similar talk that Reaper did. "Son you always choose girls that get your ass beat," My dad says swirling around the whiskey in his glass. "What does that mean?" Reaper asks curiously. "Last year he went out with a girl who ended up being a gang leader's daughter, so that got him his ass beat and a couple of months ago we slept with a girl who ended up being another gang leader's girlfriend, so that was also a bloody week," My dad explains as I continue glaring at him, to which the rest of the men just laugh...

Hadera's POV

"So when is the date?" Mom asks as I sit down my face still heated from blushing so much. "*He says tomorrow but I don't know what we're doing,*" I answer taking small glances toward Samual. "*Don't worry I'll ask him so I can dress you up accordingly*" Judith says, a giddy smile on her face. We continue to talk until Uncle Don called church for all the members and Old ladies, leaving Judith and I alone. "*Why don't you go get changed and then we can go have a bit of fun,*" She says mischievously. I nod cautiously, heading upstairs to my room and putting on my bear onesie.

I remove my makeup and wash my face then head back downstairs to see Judith with a bottle of wine and two glasses. *Are you sure we should be doing this, you aren't even 16 yet?* I ask as she continues to pour wine into both glasses. "Its fine wine will make me tipsy anyway," she says finishing up the last glass and handing me one. I set eh glass down and sign, *I'm not sure, I've never drank before.* Judith's eyes widen hearing my confession before signing, *There's a first time for everything Angel, and drink up,* she says then taking a sip of the wine. I take my first sip of the wine and it wasn't so bad it was sweet but at the same time, it was pretty bitter. We continue drinking and taking breaks in between to sign, we soon finish the first bottle and move on to the next...and maybe one more bottle after that.

Soon enough I was practically drunk and Judith was mostly tipsy almost drunk, Judith is what you would consider a happy crazy stupid drunk, she tried balancing things on her head and she also raided the fridge. I'm more of an emotional drunk, out of nowhere I started crying when I found out that someone had eaten my stash of chips. *"Someone ate my chips,"* I say letting out a choked sob as tears started falling down my face. I could tell Judith was laughing at me, I started screaming and chasing her around the bar, occasionally knocking down some chairs. I guess we were making a to of noise because soon enough all the club members and old ladies came out of the church room with confusion on their faces.

I caught up to Judith tackling her to the ground right in front of everyone as she continued to laugh at me. I was too busy trying to Kill Judith so I didn't notice dad and Uncle Don yelling at me to stop. "I KNEW IT YOU ATE MY CHIPS DIDN'T YOU! ADMIT IT" I yell putting Judith in a chokehold as she tries to roll from under me. Dad and Uncle Don eventually ripped us away from each other, Judith was still laughing while I started crying. I hugged dad and continued crying about my now eaten chips.

Samual's POV

"We found out who ordered the shooting," My dad says to everyone, I didn't miss the sad look on his face as he said it. "It was the Fire Souls MC and Sam's mother," Uncle Don says giving me a sympathetic look. I haven't seen my mother since I was 1 why would she want revenge on my dad or me. "That doesn't make sense why would she want any of us dead?" I ask rather harshly, "It's because she hates that your father didn't make her his old lady and that he took her son," Jesus says, his arms crossed over his chest as he glares at the wall.

"But why now it's been years since that," Dario asks looking at my dad. "Maybe she didn't have the resources then but she does now," Dad says, Hacker then projects his computer onto the screen int he from showing a map, "There clubhouse is right here in Tampa, Florida, they own various businesses, night clubs, country clubs, restaurants, and even a few underground brothels, Maryland (Sams mom) is married to their president, Rigg, and they don't have any children," Hacker finishes showing a picture of my 'mom' and her husband.

"Ah Fuck, how did that make that, you defiantly take after your father," Dario said as the picture of my 'mom' popped on the screen. "She did not look like that all those years ago, she had a bunch of surgeries but most of them were botched," Hacker says pulling up her medical history. "Why does that guy look like he drinks Mountain dew for breakfast and lives in a trailer home," Dario asks his face morphed into one of disgust the more he looks at the bother of them. "She downgraded," Jesus says making a gagging face. "She did," I mumbled taking in the fact that I technically have a stepfather. We continued discussing our next moves when we heard chairs falling and screaming. We all make out way outside to see my Angel chasing a laughing Judith around the bar, knocking over chairs and screaming. She finally tackled Judith but sadly it was right in front of all of us.

"YOU ATE MY CHIPS I KNOW YOU DID! ADMIT IT!" Angel yelled as loud as she could as Judith continued giggling. Angel put her in a chokehold for a good few seconds before Uncle Don and Reaper ripped them away from each other. My angel started crying into Reaper's chest mumbling about chips and practically having a full breakdown over them. Reaper tried calming down Hadera while Judith just laughed and said, "Woohooo I fEeL sO A-aLiVe," slurring her words and collapsing into her fathers chest, she was out cold. "What the hell?!" Aniya says as she walks over to the bar. "THEY DRANK MY GOOD WINE!" she yells holding up 3 bottles of Livio Sassette Brunello di Montalcino. Everyone looked terrified for the girls because Aniya doesn't play when it comes to her wine. "I'm s-sorry mom," Hadera says her quiet voice says with tears still in her eyes. "You know what it's ok I'm just glad you're breaking some rules, not a lot of parents want their children to break rules but honey you are too angelic for this world," Aniya says walking up to her daughter and engrossing her in a loving hug.

I helped Hadera to her bed seeing as t was almost 3 in the morning and we'd been up since the party. I could tell she was exhausted so she fell asleep pretty quickly, I went into her bathroom looking for ibuprofen leaving it on her nightstand and moving her trash can next to her side of the bed. I leave a small kiss on her forehead before standing up to leave, just as I was about to leave Hadera's small hand grabs mine and mumbles 'stay' not letting go of my hand. I remove my shirt and shoes before climbing into bed with her, pulling her small body onto my chest...

# Chapter 11: Hangovers and Kisses

Hadera's POV

I was awoken by a wave of nausea causing me to keel over my bed letting out the contents of my stomach. My head was pounding and my throat raw from throwing up, my eyes still closed not noticing that Samual was slowly waking up, I felt another wave of nausea cause me to start dry heaving, and tears well up in my eyes. I could feel Smauals warm hand rubbing my back as I continue dry heaving, he helps me out of bed to the bathroom. I wash out my mouth and take the pain pills that he left on my nightstand, I go into my closet choosing a comfy outfit for the day. I barely make it back to bed before I collapse on my bed, my headache still not settling down.

"C-can you help me get dressed," I ask probably almost whispering, Sam helps me sit up as he helps me undress, as soon as the top of my onesie was off I quickly went to cover my chest, embarrassed that we wouldn't like my body because I was rather skinny.

Sam puts two fingers under my chin lifting my gaze to meet his as he says, "You look beautiful," he slowly moves my hands from my chest and leans down leaving three kisses on my chest the last one on my heart. This made me blush knowing that I've never been touched or even kissed in this way before. He continues helping me remove my clothes keeping his eyes strictly on my eyes not letting them wander. He helps me put on a white undershirt and then helps me into my grey Nike sweats. I follow him into the hall and then into his room where he goes into the bathroom to change into an almost identical outfit to mine. "Let's get you something to eat," he says leading me downstairs where everyone except for Judith and Damien sat.

Sam gets me breakfast and checks up on me now and then, "*What about our date,*" I ask as he checks up on me for the 5th time in the last hour. "Don't worry we're just gonna have a picnic in the back of the clubhouse," he says kissing me on the forehead as he walks back towards the rest of the men. *He likes you* Mom signs with a giddy smile on her face, I playfully glare at her and we all continue talking till we see Judth walking downstairs with the help of Damien. "*Hi everyone,*" she says sitting in the booth next to mom. *You look like crap,* I sign cringing at the last word, "*Hey you let me open the wine!*" she exclaims trying to blame her choices on me. I give her a playful glare before signing, *Your the one who suggested it and I didn't even want to I had never drank before* I say exposing her and her lie. Everyone laughs at our little playful argument, and we continue to talk for hours until Sam comes over and says "Read for our date?". I nod as the aunts and mom giggle, he leads me outside where there is already a blanket on the floor with a basket of food. We sat down and talked, taking breaks to eat, Sam feed me strawberries and I'd feed him occasionally too.

"What are your plans for after high school?" He asks, with a bit of fear in his eyes, I guess he doesn't want me to go far for college or move away. "*I planned on going to a college in the near states or here, maybe South Carolina or Georgia State, although my dream college is New York School of Music, I'm not sure I could be far away for that long,*" I said shrugging, "Africa?" He asks I could tell his mood got damper by the minute "*Even if I went to Stellenbosch I'd still want to be with you,*" I reply caressing his cheek. He shows a soft smile before our eyes lock, and our lips slowly get closer before he impatiently slams his lips into mine. The kiss wasn't hungry nor was it showing any sign of sexual progression, the kiss was passionate, sweet, and loving. We pull away panting, he rests his forehead on mine and closes his eyes, I do the same as we sit there for a few minutes till he kisses my forehead and I lean my head on his chest, my eyes getting heavier and heavier until I was out like a light...

Sam's POV

Her lips were softer than I could've imagined, my little angel is the most important person in my life as of now, and I can't bear to see her leave for college out of the country. But if she did I'd support her no matter what, if she wants to go to college on the moon then so be it. I carry a sleeping Hadera into the clubhouse and up to her room, I could feel everyone's gaze on us as I carried her. After tucking her into her bed I head back downstairs to see the men nursing beers and the women drinking wine and gossiping. "What's got you so distressed?" Damien asks handing me a beer, "Hadera was talking about what she wanted to do after high school and she mentioned maybe going to college in New York," I say sadly. "New York! She's never said anything about going to college out of state," Reaper says, a distressed look playing on his face.

"Face guys Hadera is growing up, this would have happened eventually, New York has the best music schools in the country," Jesus says shrugging it off like it's nothing. "We will miss her if she does go but she can always visit and call," My dad says grabbing another beer from behind the bar. "Yeah, I guess," I say agreeing, Hadera can go to the moon and id still follow her, music makes her happy and that's what I want to do, make her happy, even in it means having her move a few states away...

# Chapter 12: Kidnapping



It was probably the middle of the night when I felt vibrations on the room floor, I knew Sam had slept in his room tonight so I doubt it was him, the footsteps were a lot heavier than my dad's steps but they could be any one of my uncles. Whoever it was had knocked down papers from my desk and ripped the sheets off my bed. Just as I turned to look at who was in the room a hand came over my mouth muffling my scream. The man picked me up as if I was as light as a baby, tossing me over his shoulder harshly making his way out my window and towards a black van. I scream and squirm trying to get out of his grip but it was no use he throws me in the van hitting my head on a box. Tears roll down my face as pain pulses through my body. The same man grabs a damp cloth putting it on my face before I had time to scream I was out like a light...

3rd person POV

The clubhouse was still and quiet, nobody was awake, and it seemed like a normal morning to everybody. Everyone woke up at the usual time, ate breakfast joked, and some went to work. "Where's Hadera?" Reaper asked Sam as he was always the one to be with her, "I don't know ill go check her room," he replies heading upstairs thinking of what adorable sleeping position Hadera would be in. Sam rang the doorbell and entered the room to see Hadera's room in a mess, her sheats were barely on the bed, papers were scattered throughout the room, and her window looked as if it was pried open with a crow bar. "DAD, UNCLE DON, REAPER, GET UP HERE," Sam yells looking about the window to see tire tracks and boot tracks. "What happened?" Reaper asked, stopping to look at the ransacked room. "What the fuck!" Aniya yells as she looks at her daughter's room. Sam walks over to her bed seeing a note left on her bed, "Dear Dean, I hope you realized your mistake when you left me and took the brat with you, since you took something from me I'm taking something from your son, the little deaf bitch will make a fun toy for my husband's men -Maryland," Sam read out loud his voice wavering as a single tear falls down his cheek. His beautiful Angel is gone, and he couldn't stop them from taking her...

Reapers POV

"Get everyone ready we're going to Tampa right now!" I yell running to my room and grabbing my gun, knives, and keys. I walk downstairs to see all the men ready to go, Alana and Dario were getting medical supplies if needed, and Kai was strapping his weapons onto his belt. "Ok, everyone it will take us 6 hours to get to their clubhouse I want everyone alert we've never had to go to war with this club, we don't know how they think or what they know," Prez says as we all walk outside and mount our bikes. Aniya runs over to me and gives me a quick kiss and hug as we start our bikes and get ready to ride.

Time Skip

We managed to make it to Tampa by the late afternoon, Prez went over the plan and showed us a schematic of their clubhouse and showed us any place where they would keep my daughter. I could tell Hazard was trying his hardest to keep his emotions in check, I knew he loved my daughter and I'm surprisingly happy about it. He's patient and doesn't treat her any different than a hearing person, he knows she's smart and not so innocent as everyone thinks. "This isn't your fault you wouldn't have known, and I know Hadera doesn't blame you," I say putting a comforting hand on Hazard's shoulder. He only nods as we get ready to sneak into their clubhouse. There weren't many bikes in front of the clubhouse, so that means most of them are out.

We barge into the clubhouse scaring the members that were inside, they all looked as if they lived off beer and cigarettes, the place reeked of BO, smoke, and cheap beer. "What the hell are ya'll doing!" one man yells, "We're here for my daughter!" I spit outpointing the gun at his head. "You mean the little deaf bitch? That girl ain't going nowhere!" he yells attempting to pull out his gun, I shoot him before he was a chance. The whore on his lap screaming and trying to run away but gets stopped by some of our men.

Hazard and Kai make their way toward the basement while the rest of us go looking for Rigg and Maryland. We make our way upstairs to hear moaning coming from the last door marked president on the door. I smirk and kick the door down King, Prez and I walk in to see Maryland and Rigg going at it on his desk. Maryland screams like a little bitch and tries to run but gets stopped by King, "Funny seeing you here, I knew you were a bitch but I didn't think you were a psycho!" He yells grabbing her hands and tying the together and sitting her on the floor. "Well if it isn't King, Don, and Reaper it's been a while," Rigg says pulling his pants back up. "What is your head possessed you to take My daughter!" I yell out grabbing him by the collar. He smiles cockily before replying "Your little deaf daughter makes a good toy for my men, so innocent, pure, that little mouth of her ca-" I cut him off by punching his face, I punched him till his face was swollen. We drag him and Maryland out of the clubhouse tossing them in the club van. I run back inside to see if the boys found Hadera. As I arrive I see them carrying Hadera, she was unconscious, her face swollen and bruised, she was in Hazard's shirt...

Hadera's POV (Trigger)

I had only been here less than a day and my whole body was in pain. Men constantly came into the cell to either beat me or violate me. All I wanted was Sam, I wanted his kisses, his cuddles, his love, Not these horrible men. I knew my family would come for me, they wouldn't leave me alone. "If it isn't the little bitch," A dyed blond woman with a spray tan and horrible botched botox and lip fillers says as she walks into the cell. "I don't know what my son sees in you, you're just a little deaf whore," she says making sure I read her lips. "s-so your S-sams mom, you know I've heard you used to be pretty, but now you look botched as hell," I say trying not to wince in pain, I smirk as her face fills with anger. She grabs a knife from the tray next to her and just started cutting me, yelling even though I can't hear her.

Time skip

It's been hours since my body was cut up, a man had come in almost an hour ago and hadn't left he was groping my breasts and kissing my lips and neck. I was crying and screaming this was the longest any of the men had been in here. As he was about to put his hand in my underwear he was ripped off of me by Kai! "K-kai!" I yell out sobbing seeing my brother beat the man up until he's unconscious...

Kai's POV

The basement was horrible, the cells were dirty and filled with corpses, and it reeked of burning flesh and blood. "What the hell!?" Hazard screams as he looks into the last cell, Hadera lay half-naked screaming with a man on top of her, he was groping her and kissing her. I ripped the man off her beating him to a pulp until he was unconscious. "K-kai!" I hear Hadera yell, I look up seeing my little sister trying to cover her bloody chest with her hands. Hazard runs in taking off his shirt and we help her put it on. I could tell she was in a lot of pain but Hazard picks her up anyway giving her a soft kiss on her lips. "Let's get you out of here," Hazard says as we run out of the clubhouse.

"D-dad!" Hadera yells seeing our dad run back into the building. "What happened?" He asked seeing her in Hazard's shirt and no pants. "We'll explain later," Hazard says sadly as his hand caresses her back. We take Hadera to the second van where Alana is waiting in to treat her wounds. She gives Hadera a sedative to help her with pain and knock her out so Alana can stitch up her wounds "Now can you tell me what happened?" Dad asks arms crossed over his chest. "We found her all cut up with a man on top of her groping and kissing her," Hazard says looking down not wanting the meet my father's gaze. Dad punches the side of the van leaving dent after dent. King and Uncle Don hold my father back from damaging the van before saying to time to go so we mount our bikes and start them up...

# Chapter 13: Epiloge

Hadera's POV (3 months later)

It's been 3 months since I was kidnapped and I have to admit it's been the best 3 months of my life. I graduated a year early and I was offered a scholarship to the New York School of Music, Sam had asked me to be his girlfriend last month, and it couldn't have been in a better way possible.

Flash Back

It had been 2 months since the kidnapping I have been going to therapy twice a week for my nightmares. Sam has been by my side every step of the way. He moved into our clubhouse shortly after the incident wanting to make sure I was ok. He asked me to meet him in the music room today, I enter the music room to see a smiley Sam holding something behind his back. "*What's behind your back?*" I ask trying to see behind him making him turn. "Close your eyes," he says and I comply. I feel him place something fluffy in my hand. I open my eyes to see a little bear holding a heart asking "Be Mine?"

Like this but it says Be Mine? instead

"So will you Be Mine?" He asks sheepishly, I could tell he's nervous. I nod before screaming "YES!"

Flashback Over

It was an adorable way to ask me to be his girlfriend a bit cheesy but cute. Not being his girlfriend is amazing but I don't know how to tell him about the scholarship all I can hope is for the best. "*Babe, can I talk to you?*" I ask as he sits on my bed playing a game on his phone. "Of course angel," he replies putting his phone away and giving me his undivided attention. "So I got a letter yesterday saying that I was accepted into the New York School of Music on a full scholarship, and I accepted," I say showing him the paper. Sam sits there for a second taking in the new information before a smile spreads over his face. "That's amazing!" he yells out engulfing me in a hug and leaning in to give me a soft yet passionate kiss. "I will support you no matter

what, even if it means leaving the club for a while. And that's just
what he did, Sam moved to New York with me...

www.ingramcontent.com/pod-product-compliance
Lightning Source LLC
Chambersburg PA
CBHW071356200726

48294CB00004B/1186